First published in 2005 in Great Britain by
Barrington Stoke Ltd, Sandeman House, Trunk's Close,
55 High Street, Edinburgh EH1 1SR

ISBN 1-842992-96-1

Printed in Great Britain by Bell & Bain Ltd

A Note from the Author

Do you know what people say? That "truth is stranger than fiction"? Well, I believe that 100%.

Most of my ideas come from things that really happen. But the story behind *Exit Oz* was very, very close to home.

You see, I have two teenage sons. They're like the brothers in this book, and they have a pet snake. He's called Oz. Just like Oz in this story. And, just like Mum in this story, I'm not too keen on him!

When Oz was a few months old he vanished down the sink overflow while my sons were giving him a bath.

Exactly as I tell you in the story ...

I'm always on the lookout for true stories I can steal to turn into books. It's great fun to write this way because then your stories begin with real roots. You can use them to make characters and events that are larger than life. I hope you enjoy reading *Exit Oz* as much as I enjoyed writing it!

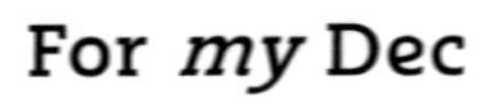
For *my* Dec

Contents

Chapter 1
Meet Oz

I blame Jock, the pet shop owner, for what happened to Oz.

I like to go into Jock's shop every Saturday to check out the snakes. His pythons are the best. I want one, but Mum says, "Dream on, Declan."

So I visit them instead.

Jock knows me so well now he lets me handle his snakes if the shop's quiet. I love the heavy, sleepy, silky way they curl themselves up my arm.

Snakes aren't slimy and damp or cold, by the way. People who've never held a snake think they are. But no. Snakes are dry and cool. They feel smooth next to your skin. I wouldn't mind looking after the big python from Jock's shop for a while. Petula the Python – that's what Jock calls her. It would be great to feel her slither from one of my hands into the other all day long. And all the time, Jock could be telling me some new fact about snakes. Things I didn't know before.

"Snakes really like water, you know. Most of all when they're shedding their skins, like Oz," was one of Jock's Facts of the Week.

And that's why I blame him for what happened. Sort of.

When I gave Oz his treat, I thought I was doing OK. It seemed the right thing to do just then.

Oz is *my* pet snake, by the way.

He's not a huge long snake like a boa constrictor.

He's not even a python.

I wish.

He's just a wee corn snake.

You can call Oz a rat snake too. His proper scientific name is *elaphe guttata*. But I think *corn snake* sounds better. I'll stick to calling him that.

Oz is 8 months old.

40 cm long.

About as thick as a ball-point pen.

He has red-brown marks all over him, with black rings round them, like the spots on a giraffe.

Beautiful, he is.

Harmless.

Non-venomous. No poison in his fangs.

Oz is the *only* kind of snake my mum will let me have. And she'll only let me have the one snake.

Ever.

Mum thinks one snake in the house is *quite* enough.

She's *fed up* seeing Oz slithering and side-winding over the kitchen table while she's eating.

Or stuck in her hair for a laugh.

Or outside his tank *anywhere*.

Because he might escape.

AGAIN!

Escape – that's what Oz did when I was giving him his treat. The wriggly wee chancer!

I thought Oz needed a treat because it can't be much of a life being a pet corn snake.

You live in a plastic tank in someone's bedroom. Or – if you're Oz – you live in a plastic tank in two people's bedrooms. Oz spends one week looking at the bands in all my rock posters. Plus, he gets to listen to heavy metal music and my awesome drumming. That's when he's living in my room. Then the next week in Gabe's room he's got all these moody black walls around him and sad music and the honk of joss sticks.

Maybe Oz would like a bit of Country and Western instead of Ozzy Ozbourne. After all, he is an American corn snake. But there's no way he's going to get the chance to find out. I'm not playing him that crap!

I feel sorry for Oz sometimes, but not that sorry.

That's the problem with being a snake.

If you're not happy about something you can't make a fuss. You don't bark or growl or chew the table legs. You don't need to go for walks, so you're pretty much left alone. Day in, day out.

If you're lucky, and your humans remember, you get fresh newspaper to poo on. But it's not as if you can even *read* the sports pages to pass the time while you do your business. The only good thing in your **life** is your weekly meal!

Yes, that's right. I said WEEKLY.

That's when you get your pinky.

Your pinky, by the way, is nothing to do with cute little fingers and toes. A pinky—

Hang on.

I know how dweeby some people are so I'd better put this in before I say any more ...

Warning for Wimps!

Do not turn the page if what you are about to read will make you feel sick.

OK? No wimps still reading?

Right.

A pinky is a teeny tiny baby mouse.

Not a sugar mouse.

A dead baby mouse.

You call it a pinky because it's got no hair yet so you see all its bare pinky skin. Doesn't have eyes either. Just two wee slits where eyes would grow if the pinky wasn't just snake food – a baby mouse that's bred to be killed as soon as it's born.

When one time I asked Jock how the pinkies were killed he didn't look at me. Just muttered, "With a needle in the heart".

OK. So I know all this sucks for the pinky but it's lucky for people who keep snakes. It means I don't have to creep about looking for mice nests and stealing live mouse babies to feed to Oz. I'm no wimp but even *I* don't fancy any of that carry-on!

And, yeah, if you must know, I *do* think it's a bit ... well, *sad*, when I go to buy the pinkies. You get them in the pet shop.

Frozen, like ice-lollies. Or oven chips.

They come in bags of ten, cuddled up to each other like they're cold or scared. I have to break them apart to put them in this special box that goes in our freezer. It has a label on it that says **MICE!!!!!!!!** Mum gave me the box when she found out about what Oz has to eat. The box is all white and the label is **huge**. You can't see what's inside.

Mum's a total *woose* about the pinkies. She won't even *look* at them, and can't stay in the kitchen when I'm getting a pinky out for Oz to eat. All I need to do is rattle the **MICE!!!!!!!!** box at her and she's off with her hands over her eyes.

"Don't show me. It's dis-**GUST**-ing!" Mum squeaks and squeals. She sounds like a little mouse herself.

There's nothing yuk to see anyway. Pinkies are cute wee things really. They're about the size of a square of chocolate, but – and I'm guessing here – maybe more chewy and crunchy and not as sweet ...

Unless you're a snake, that is.

One pinky is enough to keep a young snake going for up to SIX weeks.

Can you imagine?

Only *one* square of Dairy Milk in six weeks for a growing snake?

But it's true – Oz went *five weeks* without his pinky when he had the adventure I'm going to tell you about.

Before I start telling you about it, I've one more eeky pinky fact for you –

You can't feed frozen pinkies to your pet snake.

Well, *you* don't eat your curry or your fish and chips ice-cold or brick-hard, do you?

So, you defrost the pinky in a mug of boiling water. In our house, anyway. In "a *special* mug, that human lips", Mum says, "must never, *ever* touch again."

MICE MICE MICE she made me paint in black nail varnish all round Oz's *special* mug. I had to do that because of Gabe. Gabe made Mum a cuppa in that mug because she wouldn't let him paint his wooden floor **black black black** to go with his nails and his hair and his clobber and his life ...

Gabe was careful *not* to wash the mug out just after we'd defrosted the pinky. He chucked a teabag into the hot water where the pinky had been.

Mum barfed *everywhere* when Gabe told her what he'd done.

Of course, Gabe thought it was hilarious. He would!

Chapter 2
Gabe!

Gabe.

I have to talk about him for two reasons –

1. He's my big brother.

2. There's no getting away from him in this story, even though he's a bigger pain than a boil on your bahooky!

Mum says Gabe's named after an angel – Gabriel. She's got to be joking!

Gabe says his tag's Gabe the Goth. If you ask me he looks more like a very ugly, spotty girly to me! He's all sooty black eyes and floaty black clothes. He wears a leather dog collar with studs all over it that he bought from *my* pet shop. The only cheery things about Gabe are the millions of jingly silver bangles he wears up his arms and a bright red DEATH ROCKS tattoo on his zitty butt that Mum hasn't seen ...

Yet.

Don't worry – I'm just waiting for the perfect moment to grass.

I mean, bangles? Make-up? What's that all about?

Because I'm *normal*, I try and keep away from Gabe, but he always ends up sticking his nose into what I'm doing. He mucks everything up. Totally.

I wouldn't be telling you *any* of this if Gabe hadn't messed everything up.

Oz would have had his bath.

Shed his skin.

End of story.

Except ...

It was **Gabe's** bright idea to take Oz to the water instead of bringing the water to Oz.

And I had to go along with him.

Not just because Gabe's older and bigger and wider and meaner and louder than I am.

It's because he's got *rights*.

See, I said Oz was *my* pet snake. That's only half true. He's half Gabe's, too.

That's why the poor little reptile – I mean Oz, not Gabe – has to spend half his life in a black room.

He has to sniff the joss sticks and tune into the vibe of Marilyn Manson and the Velvet Underground whether he likes it or not.

No wonder Oz hides under his wooden log all day long when he's living with Gabe. No wonder he stays curled up in a ball! I bet he's thinking, *Let me outa here*! Oz doesn't have any eardrums to cover or hands to cover them with. I'm lucky. That's what I do whenever I go into Gabe's room.

And that's what I was planning to do as soon as I came home from the pet shop. I wanted to do what Jock said and get Oz straight into some warm water. I wanted to give Oz a treat.

See, it was Gabe's week to have Oz. I dug around in the kitchen cupboards for an old dish to use as a bath so Mum wouldn't freak out and I wondered how I was even going to get past the –

KEEP OUT

OR

YOU DIE, DEC

(I MEAN IT!)

– welcome sign painted on the door of Gabe's room. It was under an evil skull and crossbones sign.

I had to be brave. After all, I was going to do something good. I was going to help my helpless little pet.

"Do something good. Help your helpless little pet. Be brave, Dec," I chanted to myself and I poured some water into an old *Snap! Crackle! Pop!* bowl I'd found. Then I knocked on Gabe's door.

"Jock said pet snakes can have problems shedding," I'd say if Gabe strangled me for coming near his room. "We've got to bath Oz in warm water. Rub off the bits of his skin that are stuck ..."

I was planning how I'd say all this and survive.

I stared at that skull and crossbones sign.

I gulped.

"Gabe?" I called in my cheeriest voice.

There was silence.

No gloomy music playing.

Hmm. Maybe Gabe was trying to write one of his Death Songs. Gabe has a band. The Nothings, they're called. He says he's the singer. If he's a singer I'm King of the Moon!

"Gabe?" I called again. This time I made my voice sound as friendly as I could.

Still silence.

Maybe Gabe was busy. Sewing black words like

DEATH

HELL

NOTHING IS EVERYTHING

on one of his black T-shirts.

No, I thought. *He's not sewing.* Gabe always plays dismal, gloomy music when he does his needlework.

My hands were full with the bowl of water, so I gave Gabe's door a kick.

"Gabe? Can I check Oz?" I shouted.

Silence!

"All right!" I whooped.

Just me and Oz, I thought. *House to ourselves!*

Mum at the shops, Dad at the footy, Gabe was ...? I didn't care where Gabe was!

"Got a treat for you, Ozzy-Wozzy," I yelled now. I went into Gabe's room. I didn't care about the water that I sloshed all over his floor as I put the bowl down.

Then I checked his underwear drawer for my missing Calvin boxers. There they were! Yuck – I'd need to boil wash them now! I thought I'd pay Gabe back for nicking them so I mopped up the puddles on the floor with his beloved KURT IS KING T-shirt. Then I lifted Oz from his tank.

Oz felt so thin and light after the giant pythons Jock had let me handle earlier that morning. Petula was so heavy. When she'd coiled round my wrist, she'd made all the veins bulge on my hand. Then she'd squeezed them hard.

Oz was trying to do the same thing. He was squeezing my wrist as he twisted around it, but his hold was looser than one of Gabe's bangles.

"Bath time, Ozzy," I said. Now that Oz was out of his tank, he stretched his neck up at me. His head darted and ducked to and fro in front of my face. That forked tongue of his vibrated so fast I couldn't see it. It was blurred like the end of a ruler when you ping it –

Boyoyoiiiiiinnnnggggg!!!

Faster than the speed of sight!

That's how Oz smells. He uses his tongue to pick up everything that's in the air. The smells get carried to a special opening in the roof of his mouth called Jacobson's organ.

OK. You might not want to know that now, but *one* day you might be on *Who Wants to be a Millionaire?*

That might be the *last* question between you and a million smackers – "What is Jacobson's organ?"

And now the answer's stored in your head – thanks to me –

It's D, Chris. Jacobson's organ lets snakes smell. Final answer!

Anyway, back to reality.

I held Oz up to my face.

"You're lovely," I told him, and his eyes glittered at me like black diamonds. He *is* lovely, by the way, beautiful markings, perfect head. But even I had to admit that for the last few days he hadn't looked his best.

There was a milky film over his eyes, so they weren't as glittery as they could be. And Oz'd been having a few bad skin days. So his scales were dull. Worse than that, they were flaking off in patches. Oz was shedding, you see. Or trying to.

Every few weeks, Oz's body grows too tight for his outer skin. Then he needs to burst out of it. It's happened six times since

Oz was a new hatchling. There hadn't ever been a problem before. Oz had just rubbed and rubbed his head against the log in his tank until he broke a hole in his old skin. Then his body would slip out of it. The old skin got left behind in the tank like a papery tube. Then I could show off the old skin to my mates while Oz preened in his tank, showing off his glossy new self to me. It was as if he was saying, *I'm looking fan-tastic!*

This time round that hadn't happened. In this shedding, bits of Oz's old skin were stuck to his body. The old skin looked like cracked varnish on old wood. It wasn't a pretty sight! But that didn't bother me. What upset me was the thought that Oz might be in pain as his shedding went wrong.

Jock in the pet shop said I could help Oz shed by putting him into warm water and letting him soak.

So now, here I was, taking Oz from the tank above Gabe's bed. "In you go for your bath, Oz," I said softly. His tail was just dipping the water when Gabe's black duvet twitched.

And spoke to me.

Chapter 3
Exit Oz

"Didn't you read the warning on the door?"

This was freaky. The duvet was alive and it sounded *so* like Gabe.

Dangerous.

Angry.

Bigger than me.

It even jangled like the bangles on Gabe's arms.

There were a few seconds as I dangled Oz over his bowl when I thought that Gabe must be one clever Goth! Had he hidden motion sensors round his room to catch unwanted visitors? Was his voice on a tape somewhere that got switched on to scare them?

Wow!

I was impressed ... till the duvet twitched again. It rose in the air. Landed on my head. It seemed to have arms. They were at my throat.

Gabe the Goth hadn't been clever at all. He just hadn't bothered getting up. It was Saturday, after all. Sometimes, at weekends, he sleeps all day long like a very lazy vampire. Well, it's not as if he has a girl to spruce up for. The only girls Gabe meets are in his dreams.

No wonder he wasn't happy with me.

"What ya doin'?" Gabe growled. He guffed out stinky breath in my face. Then he spotted the cereal bowl on the floor.

"And that's *my* bowl. I saved up six tokens for that! Give!" he said. He snatched up the bowl. The water in it soaked his spotty chest.

"Oi! You're dead already," Gabe seethed. His bangled arm lifted high to scud me one.

So I had to move fast. And talk faster. It's a skill younger brothers have to develop.

"Oz needs a bath," I said, ducking to dodge Gabe's arm again. "He's not well."

Big brothers are strange. I mean, on the one hand Gabe could easily have killed me in cold blood for putting a single toe into his bedroom. With a heart of stone he'd watched his poor *mother* drink from a cuppa floating with pinky slime. He'd even tried to pierce his own nipple with a blunt safety pin ... Yet on the other hand he was a softy, a total marshmallow about his teddies, and his Winnie the Pooh posters, his *Snap! Crackle! Pop!* bowl ... *and* his pet serpent.

"Sick?" Gabe bleated. "Ozzy is sick?"

One minute Gabe was karate chopping my belly so hard I snapped forward at the waist like a penknife shutting. The next moment, Gabe was lifting Oz *ever* so kindly from my hands.

"Whassa matta, baby?" he cooed, blowing kisses. "Tell dada!"

"Oz can't talk," I gasped. "But he needs a bath."

"So what are we waiting for?"

This is why I mean it was Gabe's fault for making what happened to Oz a story.

While I was carefully checking if any of my ribs were broken, Gabe was already in the bathroom next door. With Oz. I could hear water running. Gabe was filling the sink.

"What you doing?" I shouted, hurling myself into the bathroom.

"Whassit look like? Eatin' pizza," Gabe sneered. He held Oz up to his face to share his *I'm so funny* snigger. His free hand was testing the heat of the water in the sink. He looked like a mummy about to bath her baby.

"You can't put him in *there*," I cried, reaching for Oz.

"Gonna stop me?" Gabe growled. He looked hard at me with his sooty eyes. Then he went all mushy again.

"I'm gonna put you in a *big* bath, baby," Gabe explained to Oz even though snakes don't speak Human. Gabe was using the smoochy voice he used on the phone to try and make girls forget he was Shrek's identical twin.

Ugh!

Now he was *pouting* at Oz. Honestly, it'd make you chuck your Cheerios, the sight of Gabe's blubber lips blowing kisses at anything, even a snake. No wonder Oz stretched out his neck, turned his head in disgust and tugged through Gabe's fingers at me.

Get me outa here, Dec! his wee face seemed to say.

I'd be the same if a prat like Gabe was trying to slip me the tongue!

"Oz wants *me*. You're scaring him," I told Gabe. I took Oz quickly in both hands and let him down towards the water.

"No chance. He's mine this week, not yours." Gabe had his fingers round my wrists. His grip felt really tight and hard for a guy who wears so much make-up.

"Jock told *me* what to do—"

"No way. *I'm* bathing Oz—"

It was while Gabe and I were busy bickering that I felt Oz unfurling inside my cupped hands.

I wonder if he suddenly thought –

Here's my chance! I can split from these jokers at last!

He didn't mess about, that's for sure. Saw his escape route and *Zooooom!*

I had my hands clasped over the sink, and I'd made a perfect exit hole between my thumbs and index fingers. I knew I'd made that hole, but I couldn't do anything to close it in time. *That* was Gabe's fault. He was holding me so tightly I couldn't move.

And I couldn't help thinking –

Snakes love holes.

That was the very, very first Fact of the Week Jock told me when Dad took me to buy Oz and we picked out a tank for him.

"Snakes love holes. They'll always try and escape through them. Never give them the chance," Jock had warned. And up until this moment I'd remembered Jock's advice.

I'd never given Oz the chance to side-wind away from me on a large, smooth surface so he could vanish down a space or a socket or a hole.

And I'd *always* held Oz the way Jock showed me – with both hands. It meant I could hold him more tightly if he started to wriggle free.

But now I couldn't move my hands. Gabe was gripping me so hard. When Oz poked his head through the hole I'd made he must have thought it was Corn Snake Christmas!

Yahoo! he was probably cheering – if snakes can cheer silently. Because a little way in front of him was an even *better* hole. It was bigger and darker and deeper than the sweaty boy-hole he was slipping out of ...

And faster than Gabe or I could say –

"I'm bathing Oz, ya turd—"

"No way, ya tragic loser!"

Oz's head and neck were down the overflow hole of our bathroom sink.

"Oz!" I screamed.

At last, I felt strong enough to break Gabe's grip and dive after my vanishing snake. But it was already too late.

Even though I grabbed hold of Oz, and even though Gabe put both his hands over mine and we held on together, it was too late.

One minute Oz was there, struggling in our hands, and the next ...

Well, he was gone.

Exit Oz.

We had to let him go. Oz was pulling so hard to be free that we were scared we'd hurt him if we kept tugging him back up the overflow. It felt like Oz would rip in two. Neither of us wanted that.

"Let him go, Dec," said Gabe, his voice very soft in my ear. He took his hands off mine and pulled the plug out of the sink to let Oz's bath water drain away.

"But, Gabe," I groaned. I watched the tiny point of Oz's tail fight to escape the pinch of my finger and thumb. "I'm still holding on."

"Let him go, Dec. You have to," said Gabe, and I knew he was right.

So I did.

And Oz slipped out of sight.

Chapter 4
Petless!

It felt like days passed before Gabe or I said a word.

Or moved.

Or breathed.

We both gawped at the sink. Frozen. Like a pair of pinkies with needles in their hearts. Our mouths were open. Our eyes were wide. We were petless. Oz was gone. It was horrible.

But it got worse. Gabe thumped the back of my head. I already knew what was coming next.

"That was *your* fault!" he hissed.

"It was *yours*," I shouted back, as if there was any point. Big brothers never take the blame, do they? It's their right to be right!

"You didn't hold Oz properly!" Gabe went on.

"You wouldn't let me. And *you* brought Oz into the bathroom—"

"But *you* let him go."

"You told me to!"

Gabe was moaning now. "It's your fault, Dec! He's gone."

Knowing Gabe and I, we could have spent the rest of our *lives* blaming each other for the Escape of Oz. Lucky that Mum broke things up.

"What's going on here?" she wanted to know.

Neither Gabe nor I had heard her coming home. The horror of losing Oz was too much. But she'd heard us all right!

"I could hear you from the street," she said, not sounding too chuffed.

Then came her Angry Mum Act.

"Why's this sink full of water?" she asked.

"Were you trying to dunk Dec again, Gabe?" she asked.

"Why are you so pale, Dec?" she asked.

"And why are you crying, Gabe?" she asked. "Both of you get downstairs and help me unpack the car. But let me into the loo first ..."

Poor Mum. While she spoke, she was trying to shoo us out the bathroom. I noticed she was hopping from one foot to the other.

She must have been desperate for a pee, but neither Gabe nor I budged for her. All we did was look from the mirror to the sink to each other.

Man, I *was* pale. Must have been shock. My lips were the same colour as my cheeks. They were trembling. And my whole face was milky white, like Oz's glittery eyes before we lost …

I gulped at the memory. It was all Gabe's fault.

"Mum, he put—" I began, but Gabe got there first.

"Oz is *goooooooone*," he wailed, putting on his singing voice. "Dec killed my snake."

Until that moment, I didn't know that Gabe wore blue mascara as *well* as black eyeliner, but when he started sobbing, all these inky two-tone stripes ran down his face. He looked like a panda with a broken heart, peering through the bars of a cage! I thought he was putting it all on for Mum when he threw himself to his knees, and started hitting his head off the sink. But this wasn't just an act. It was the real deal, unlike the gothy videos he made to go with his Death Songs.

"He's *goooooone.* I'll never see Ozzy again," Gabe bawled. He didn't seem to care that he looked stark raving bonkers. I'd have to tell my friends about *this* carry-on later! Where was his dignity? I don't know. Maybe you start to love your pets too much if you're 16 and no girl'll go near you. I almost felt sorry for Gabe. He was *gutted.* And don't get me wrong, I was upset too – very, *very* upset.

But I just couldn't believe we could lose Oz so easily ...

It fact, I *didn't* believe it. Maybe that's why I didn't break down like Gabe.

Not me!

I was going to get Oz back.

As I stood in the bathroom I tried to remember all those useful Facts of the Week pet shop Jock had told me.

Of course it was hard to think straight. Gabe's howls of misery were echoing off all the bathroom tiles.

"Ozzy," he was sobbing now, "you'll rot down the sink. All al*ooooone*. Or maybe you'll end up in the toilet. Oh nooooo!"

None of this was helpful when I was trying to think hard. In fact, it was totally unhelpful. Now Gabe had Mum going, too. She wasn't sad that Oz was missing. More like *terrified*.

"End up in the toilet? *Snake*?" she rasped, gawping down our lav. Her eyes bulged. "You mean I could be sitting ...? Doing a ...? And that *snake* might climb up ...? But I *really* need to go ..."

"Happy now, Dec?" Gabe snarled when Mum rushed next door to use our neighbours' loo. His voice was low but evil. "Now I'm going to have to arrange a *funeral*. And don't you *dare* think you're coming. Just remember –

"You.

Killed.

Oz."

"We don't know he's dead—" I began, but Gabe pushed me aside and slammed into his room.

At least there was peace and quiet now. Mum was next door, Gabe in his room. Horrible groany noises came from under his door as tuneless as his guitar twanging. Gabe must have started writing a new Death Song. The Goth in him would really enjoy all this sadness and gloom. And now Gabe had the chance to make me feel bad about all this for ever and ever ...

And I did feel ... well, not so much *bad* as *angry*. I should have *known* Oz would try to escape some time. That's what pet snakes do.

As I began to feel calmer I remembered what Jock had told me. Snakes scoot down a hole and sit tight. If it's cold they'll curl up. If they're shedding they won't want to move anyway. The only thing that'll bring them back out is hunger. It could take weeks ...

"Hmmm. Are you there, Oz?" I whispered into the sink.

I listened hard.

Had Oz found himself a cosy cubbyhole to shed his skin in peace? Was he coiled up, sniggering at me?

Well, down the sink or not, I wasn't giving up on him without a fight. Before there was any funeral I'd try and tempt Oz out.

With a mousetrap.

Chapter 5
The White Sink Café

My trap for Oz was not so much a snake trap as a pinky trap.

And a damn clever one, too! I thought, as I took our last four pinkies from their **Mice!!!!!!!!** box in the freezer and dropped them into their **Mice Mice Mice** mug to thaw.

I was lucky.

Mum was *still* peeing next door, so there were no tricky questions.

Like –

“Why are you defrosting so many pinkies when Oz has gone, Dec?

“And taking string upstairs, Dec?”

Mum’d *never* have let me set my trap if she’d seen me sneaking into the bathroom with a mugful of thawing mice. No chance!

And if she’d seen what I did next ...? Well, she’d have freaked. Or fainted. Or both.

See, I took the defrosted pinkies and tied a loop of string round the middle of each one. And, yes, this was a *very* slimy, squelchy, slippery job! Just you try tying string round four melting squares of Dairy Milk! That’s what it felt like, tying up those pinkies.

But I did it.

Then I tied the pinkies to the four openings on our bathroom sink.

I hung one on the spout of the hot tap.

One on the cold tap.

I put a third pinkie near the plughole. I laid that one on a square of fresh toilet paper.

After that I dangled the fourth pinky across the overflow hole which Oz had vanished down.

And there was my pinky trap.

If things went to plan, the fresh juicy mouse smells would drift down the pipes to tickle Oz's taste buds.

Yum, yum, here I come, Oz would think, if he was still down there, and ... out he'd sssssssssssssssssssnake.

How could he resist?

I knew Oz must be hungry, you see. He hadn't had anything to eat for nearly two weeks. You mustn't feed a snake when it's shedding. So, if Oz had lost his old skin during his escape, he'd be blooming STARVING! All that wriggling and rubbing that happens with shedding makes snakes very hungry. Jock told me. A snake is desperate for a scoff as soon as it's over.

But ...

(and this is where my trap was *so* sweet)

... because Oz's dinner was tied to the taps, he'd have to "sit in" and eat at The White Sink Café rather than go for a Pinky take-away. He couldn't grab his food and take it back down the pipes with him. That's when I'd catch him.

All I had to do was sit tight and wait till Oz popped out of one of the holes in the sink.

Half an hour, max, I gave him. Half an hour before he was so hungry he just had to show up and grab a mouse.

I'd let him pounce on his pinky. Curl round it. Prepare to eat.

Soon as he opened his mouth, I'd have him.

Bingo!

In case you don't know, I should tell you that it's quite something to see a snake scoff. Oz swallows his meal in one gulp. Then his *four* separate jaws get to work pushing his grub down his throat. Each jaw has to stretch itself over the pinky, like an elastic sock working its way over a wet foot! While this is happening, Oz's perfect head morphs into a mini-monster with NO table manners. My handsome corn snake turns into one evil-looking dude.

The pinky sits inside Oz's throat at first. It's a giant bulging lump, then you see it getting smaller as it moves along inside him.

Oz can hardly move while his body digests his meal. That's why I thought he'd be easy to catch if he came up the sink. While he was noshing, I'd snip the string round the pinky.

Then lift Oz out, with the pinky inside him. And tiptoe him back to his tank.

Oz would never notice that his sit-in meal at the White Sink Café was a take-away after all.

Like the best plans, mine was simple. Yet clever.

Even Gabe said so.

Well, that's a lie.

What Gabe said was, "*I* was gonna trap Oz with pinkies! You stole my idea, idiot!"

I took his insult as a huge compliment!

Chapter 6
A Song for Oz

I was sure my plan would work. Even Gabe thought it would work – if Oz was still alive, that is.

Mind you, the black **black** **black** side of Gabe was already all geared up for Oz being ***RIP***. While I'd been tying squishy pinkies to the taps, Gabe had been just as busy. While we watched over the bathroom sink, ready to grab Oz if he came up, Gabe showed me a plan of what he wanted to write on the tiles over the sink where Oz had vanished.

Like Mum would *ever* let Gabe write – "**MAY THE FORCES OF DARKNESS PROTECT YOU IN THE AFTERLIFE, MY FAITHFUL SERPENT**" on her good tiles!

Then there was the funeral itself. Gabe had been planning songs.

"Oz would have wanted 'Smells Like Teen Spirit'. I mean, he died before his time, just like Kurt," he told me. Totally serious, by the way.

Me? I was biting my tongue till it bled so I wouldn't burst out laughing. And I really couldn't control myself when Gabe added, "and we *have to* play 'Wind Beneath my Wings' while I'm lighting candles round the sink".

Oz is a snake, not a bird, I wanted to slag Gabe, but I didn't have the heart. Because poor Gabe was really putting the "M" in Mourning! Take his clobber, for example. I know, being "Gabe the Goth", everything's black already, yet he'd managed to tog up in an outfit that was *blacker* than black –

A black silk shirt (was it Mum's?),

long black gloves (they *were* Mum's!),

a black *cape* (Dad's old teacher's gown),

the cardboard top hat Gabe wore when he played the Artful Dodger in *Oliver* when he was 10 and ... wait for it ...

an old black lace scarf of my gran's. He wore this *under* the top hat, and *over* his face. All I could see through the lace were two black eyes and a pair of black lips. Total creep out!

"Will I sing my 'Song for Oz'?" the black lips asked me. "Maybe the sound of my voice'll charm him up."

Make him throw up, more like, I was thinking while Gabe's newest song echoed round our bathroom.

"You were small. You were sweet.
The coolest snake you could meet."

Gabe droned through his black lace.

The music he was strumming was a totally different tune. I think it was "She'll be Comin' Round the Mountain".

Oh, man, it was lucky I stuffed a fist in my mouth before Gabe reached the chorus of the song, because his voice went very high and shaky.

"You are gone, little serpent, you are gone,
Down the deep hole of death, you are gone.
You are gone, you are gone.
Have you have taken your last breath ...?"

There was more. Verse after verse of Gabe's "Song for Oz". I could tell you them all. But I better not. You might be reading this book for fun. I don't want to put you off going on to the end. Just like Gabe's Death Song probably put Oz off coming out!

Chapter 7
Waiting ...

Do you know what a chunk of *Bazooka Joe* bubble gum looks like when you spit it out? Dried up pinkies look the same after five days – twisted, and chewed and not very tasty-looking. *And* do they pong! A bit sweet, like a *Bazooka Joe*, but sour too. They smell like a dod of stale burger you dropped under your bed and find three weeks later.

Nasty!

So – surprise, surprise – five days after Oz escaped, Mum went ballistic. She made me take my mousetrap off the sink AND no way would she give me any money for more pinkies.

"No way, Dec!" she began, her voice getting louder. All set to get even louder.

"You want MONEY for MORE MICE and here's me running to use next door's toilet day and night because I'm scared to use my own!

"And I can't have a bath in case that snake turns up and scares the living daylights out of me.

"Poor Dad's standing in the shower in a suit washing his hands ...

"You're not washing your hands at all ...

"Gabe's had sick notes three days in a row because he says he's too sad for school ...

"And YOU want money for more mice! Get a grip, Dec!"

Of course, Mum had a point. A loud point.

Since Oz had escaped, our family life had been put on hold. Gabe wasn't eating. Mum wasn't sleeping. None of us were washing.

I knew we couldn't go on like this, but as I cleared the pinkies from the sink, I felt really, really sad.

"Sorry, Oz," I said as the dried-up, uneaten pinkies slid from my hand and plopped into the toilet bowl. Perhaps they'd bump into Oz down some smelly pipe.

"If you see him, tell Oz I did my best to get him back," I whispered, flushing the pinkies away.

From Gabe's room, I heard him wail –

"You are gone little serpent,
Never more to chew a mouse,
With your perfect mouth.
You were too good for this house."

I felt so bad, even without Gabe's "singing", that I could have flushed myself down the toilet with the pinkies. To cheer myself up I went round to the pet shop. And before you think I'm heartless, let me just say I only wanted to *look* at Jock's new-born snakes, hatchlings.

How could I *possibly* have handled another snake so soon after my own little Oz had left me? What kind of guy do you think I am?

What was the point anyway? It wasn't like Mum would let me buy one!

"Why the long face?" Jock asked as he unlocked Petula the Python's tank. While the big snake squeezed all the blood out of my arms, I told Jock my sad story.

The Escape of Oz.

The Death Song.

The Pinky Trap.

Our **Do Not Use** sink.

When I was done, Jock burst out laughing.

"What's so funny*?*" I wanted to know. This was odd. I'd been sure that Jock, of all people, would have understood how I felt about losing Oz. But he thought it was *funny*!

Jock put his hand on my arm.

"Cheer up," he said to me, "and I'll make you a bet."

I gave a shrug. I wasn't interested. Then Jock spat in his hand and put it out for me to shake. He was serious.

"You can have Petula," Jock said. "If Oz doesn't turn up in the next few weeks, she's yours. But he won't have moved far from where you lost him. Not if he was shedding."

Jock told me to get some masking tape – real strong, sticky stuff – and put it across the overflow Oz'd gone down. That, Jock said, was the most likely place he'd come up. Not the plughole or down the taps – they'd be too small for him.

"Check the tape every day," Jock told me. "And be patient. Remember, Petula's yours if Oz doesn't show."

Chapter 8
Losing my Bet

To be honest, it was Gabe who kept a check on the masking tape. He must have peeked behind it a thousand times a day.

In fact, during the next two weeks while Oz was still missing, Gabe spent most of his time in the bathroom, some of it when he should have been at school. I don't know if he *slept* there, but I do know he spent *hours* perched on the bath in his top hat and his cape and his lacy scarf, wailing his "Song for Oz". He lived on cereal eaten from his *Snap! Crackle! Pop!* bowl.

I suppose it gave him something to do. It took his mind off his spots and his greasy hair.

And in the end I have to admit that Gabe deserved to be the one who was there when Oz came back.

Which he did. Just as pet shop Jock bet me he would.

Me? I'd sort of given up on Oz after my mousetrap failed. You can call me cruel. I was already planning how to sneak a six-foot beauty called Petula up to my room without Mum finding out.

And wondering how I was going to keep a pet that lived on rats ...

I suppose I'd put Oz to the back of my mind.

Gabe never gave up like me.

And one Friday, nearly three weeks after Oz's Great Escape, he came back.

There I was in the kitchen checking out which drawer in the freezer would hide a ten-pack of rats when I heard Gabe give this *WHOOP!*

Goths don't find much to whoop about in life, but this whoop of Gabe's echoed all through the house. So I knew, even as I was running up the stairs, even as I was bursting through the bathroom door, that Oz had come home.

Jock had been spot on.

Oz *had* tried to come back the way he left – up the overflow. He was glued fast to the masking tape when Gabe peeled it back.

Apart from being pretty sticky, and – I thought – a bit thinner, Oz seemed OK, even after his adventure.

He needed a bath, mind you.

But this time, Gabe and I were taking no chances.

We found a deep bowl in the kitchen, and we put it inside a bigger bowl. We took them both into Gabe's bedroom. Then I held Oz while Gabe bathed him till he wasn't sticky.

We had to use a splash of Dad's white spirit to clean all the masking tape glue from Oz's tail. That *was* nasty! Soon as Gabe opened the white spirit, Oz tried to jump out of my hands. He wriggled like mad. He must have tasted the fumes, and he didn't like them. Didn't like the white spirit touching his tail either, but we couldn't think of anything else that would clean him properly. I was glad Gabe used the white spirit and not me. Although he looked like an undertaker working on a corpse, he was very gentle and very quick with Oz.

"Hey, Ozzy, you're brand new," Gabe said, carrying Oz back to his tank. Once Oz was safely inside, Gabe and I high-fived.

"Good job, Dec," nodded Gabe, lifting his top hat to me. I had to agree with him.

Taking care of Oz like that must have been the first time in *years* we'd done anything together without falling out!

So. I never did and I never *will* tell Gabe about the bet Jock made with me. It would break Gabe's gothy heart if he knew I'd planned to replace Oz with Petula while our little corn snake was still stuck in our sink.

And to tell you the truth, I was so glad to have Oz back, I didn't give two hoots about losing Jock's bet. In fact I even *forgot* Petula could have been mine when I burst into the pet shop to buy more pinkies.

Oz hasn't eaten for six weeks. That was all I cared about.

"Hey. So you found your snake," Jock grinned when I took my multi-pack of pinkies to his till. He waved my money away.

"This meal's on Petula and me," he said.

Chapter 9

In Case You Want to Know ...

Oz is a year and a half old now. He's twice as long as when he escaped. He hasn't pulled that stunt again, but even if he *did* fancy another adventure, he wouldn't be able to snake off down the overflow any more. He's as thick as a big stick of seaside rock (only more bendy, and better for your teeth). He's grown so much, Dad bought him a bigger tank.

There's enough room in this new tank for Oz to have his own bath. His bath's a dog bowl really with **GRUB!** written inside.

It's lucky Oz can't read. He just curls his whole self inside it and soaks there.

For anyone who wants to know about what Oz eats these days, I should tell you. Now that he's bigger, he doesn't eat pinkies any more.

Gabe and I have to feed Oz fuzz ...

Ooops.

Hang on!

Warning for Wimps, Number 2

If you think the next page is gross, stop reading <u>now</u>!!!

Gabe and I have to feed Oz fuzzies. Can you guess what they are? Do I need to explain that they're full-size *hairy* dead mice. (Geddit? – "Fuzzy")

I still buy them frozen in Jock's shop.

Still keep them in the same **MICE!!!!!!!!** box. Still defrost them in the same **MICE MICE MICE** mug. But it takes longer and – BOY! – does it freak Mum out when I shake those fuzzies at her!

Oh, and in case you're interested, feeding Oz a fuzzy is an exploding gore-fest. Blood everywhere.

Gabe can't watch. In fact, if Oz has really gone to town on his fuzzy, Gabe *pays* me to clean out Oz's tank after he's fed.

What a woose that Gabe is these days.

I wonder if it's because he's in – Wait!

Warning to anyone (even if you're not a wimp) because this is just sick!

– Gabe's in love.

With some girl he met buying bangles.

She's been in his *room* to hear his Death Song.

Can you *imagine* what poor Oz has seen going on?!?!

I bet Oz dreams of his next exit all day long.

Barrington Stoke would like to thank all its readers for commenting on the manuscript before publication and in particular:

Fady Abboud
Eliot Bentley
Sam Bridges
Fraz Chaudhry
Paul Clark
James Davies
Kenan Dole
Oliver Domleo
Kate Elliott
Vanessa Evans
Adam Gill
Jake Gould
Adam Hatton
Adam Ireland
Claire Johnson
Russell Jones
Luke Longman
Thomas Nicholls
Mitchell Norbury
Shaun Rankin
Andrew Robertson
Reece Robinson
Sam Robinson
Adam Rose-Davies
David Rowland
Verity Shingfield
Ben Smith
Oliver Soutter
Priyesh Vyas
Stephen Wong
Edward Yerburgh

Become a Consultant!

Would you like to give us feedback on our titles before they are published? Contact us at the address below – we'd love to hear from you!

Barrington Stoke, Sandeman House, Trunk's Close,
55 High Street, Edinburgh EH1 1SR
Tel: 0131 557 2020 Fax: 0131 557 6060
Email: info@barringtonstoke.co.uk
Website: www.barringtonstoke.co.uk

If you loved this book, why don't you read ...

Diary of an (Un)teenager

by Pete Johnson

ISBN 1-842991-94-9

Sunday, June 21st

"... I won't have anything to do with designer clothes, or girls, or body piercing, or any of it ... no, I shall let it all pass me by. Do you know what I'm going to be? An (Un)teenager.

But then Spencer's best mate Zac starts wearing baggy trousers and huge trainers – and even starts going on dates with girls. But Spencer is determined:
"Dear diary, I am going to stay EXACTLY as I am now. That's a promise ..."

A hilarious comedy by the "devastatingly funny Pete Johnson". *Sunday Times*